Name: Dan Fireball
Rank: Captain
Age: 12
Home planet: Earth
Most likely to: hide behind the Captain's chair and ask timidly, "Are we there yet?"

Name: Astra Moon
Rank: Second Officer
Age: 11
Home planet: The Moon
Most likely to: face up to The Geezer, strike a karate pose and say, "Bring it on!"

HS INFINITY

VOLT

Name: Volt
Rank: Agent
Age: Really old!
Home planet: Venus
Most likely to: puff steam from his shoulder exhausts and announce, "Hop completed!"

GUS

Name: Gus Buster
Rank: Head of COSMIC
Age: 15
Home planet: Earth
Most likely to: suddenly appear on the view screen and yell, "Fireball, where are you?"

Greetings new recruits!

My name is Volt and I shall be your cyber-teacher for today.

You should read this section because if you wish to become **COSMIC** agents you must know the history of the Solar System.

VOLT

Long ago, adults used to be in charge of everything. They had jobs, ran governments and were in charge of television remote controls.

Children were forced to stay in school until the age of 18. They had to do everything their parents told them. They were only given small amounts of currency, known as "pocket money".

There were lots of problems. Adults polluted the Earth and then went on to do the same — or even worse — on the remaining eight planets of our Solar System. In fact, for a long time, adults even refused to call Pluto a real planet!

So, in the year 2281, the children took over.

Adults were made to retire at the age of 18 and were sent to retirement homes on satellites in space. Children just needed three years at school, so most children were working by the time they were eight years old.

The Solar System quickly became a much happier, safer and cleaner place to live.

However, not all of the adults liked having to retire at the age of 18. Some of them rebelled and escaped from their retirement homes on satellites in space. They began to cause trouble and commit crimes.

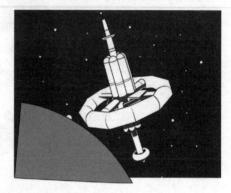

That's why **COSMIC** was created:

Crimes
   Of
      Serious
         Magnitude
            Investigation
               Company

The worst of these villains was known as The Geezer. The purpose of COSMIC was to stop The Geezer from committing crimes.

Members of COSMIC flew around the Solar System solving mysteries and bringing badly behaved adults to justice. The COSMIC spaceships could navigate an invisible series of magnetic tunnels called the Hop Field, so they were called Space Hoppers.

I myself, was a member of one such team of Space Hoppers, alongside the famous agents - Dan Fireball and Astra Moon.

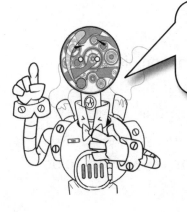

If you turn the page, you can read about a mission where The Geezer wasn't the only monster around ...

CHAPTER 1

PROFILE PICTURE

HS INFINITY DATA LOG

MISSION REPORT 8:

MONSTERS ON MERCURY

REPORT BEGINS ...

The doors to the command deck slid open and Second Officer, Astra Moon, hurried inside. "It's pouring down out there!" she moaned, grabbing a towel from her desk. "It's much too wet to work on the Hop Drive cables."

"Indeed, Miss Astra," said an old brass robot as he wheeled through the doorway behind her. Volt was also dripping wet. "If the Hop Drive had been working, we could have hopped to a planet with better weather to do the repairs."

Astra rubbed at her hair with the towel, then sat at her desk. "How's it looking, Captain?" she asked. "Are the Hop Drive readings back to normal?"

From his chair near the huge view screen at the front of the ship, Captain Dan Fireball studied the screen of his computer tablet. "Not good enough yet," he said.

 FLASH!

Suddenly, a flash of light filled the command deck.

"We finished just in time, Volt," said Astra. "Looks like there's a storm starting."

"Excuse me, Master Dan," said Volt. "Are you certain your Hop Drive readings are correct? It looks to me like the Hop Drive is mended."

 FLASH!

Another flash of light.

"Nope," said Dan. "Not quite powerful enough yet."

"Power levels look fine to me," said Astra, looking at her screen. "Have you refreshed your screen, Dan?"

"Several times," replied Dan. "I've still only got seven friends."

"I don't understand, Master Dan," said Volt.

 FLASH! ✹

Astra stood up from her seat. "That's not lightning!" she said. "It came from Dan's chair." She marched over to the Captain and grabbed the tablet from his hands.

"You're not checking the Hop Drive readings!" she exclaimed. "You're wasting time taking pictures of yourself for Spacebook!"

"It's not a waste of time!" said Dan. "Like I said, I've got seven friends already!"

"Captain Rocky Thunder?" said Astra, spotting a face she recognised near the top of Dan's friends list. "I thought you said COSMIC should never have promoted him."

"I did," said Dan. "But, this way, I can keep an eye on what he's up to and make sure he doesn't look braver than me."

"Of course," said Astra. "That's exactly what a Hop Ship Captain should spend his time doing."

"Exactly," said Dan. "The trouble is that his Spacebook profile picture is really cool. Look! He's handcuffing a bad guy. I need a better picture. Something that makes me look fearless in the face of danger. None of the ones I've taken do that."

"That's because the most dangerous thing you've done all day is play Comet Crush Saga!" snapped Astra. "Volt and I have been outside in the rain!"

The view screen at the front of the deck hissed into life and a large, serious face appeared. It was the head of COSMIC Chief Gus Buster.

"I trust your Hop Drive is now in full working order, Second Officer Moon?" he said.

"Yes, Chief!" Astra replied. "We replaced all the worn down cables with new ones."

"Good," said the Chief. "Because I need you, Captain Fireball and Volt on Mercury at once."

"Not Mercury!" moaned Dan. "It gets really hot there. It's unbearable!"

"Unbearable or not, you're going to Mercury!" growled the Chief. "Good luck, Space Hoppers. This mission could be dangerous."

Dan looked down at his Spacebook profile. "Really, sir? How dangerous?"

"Very dangerous, Captain Fireball," said the Chief. "You're going to the zoo!"

CHAPTER 2

THE ZOO

"**P**repare to Hop!" shouted Astra, then she slammed her palm down on to a large, yellow button.

The HS Infinity leapt sideways into one of the invisible magnetic tunnels that make up the Hop Field, connecting every planet and moon in the Solar System. Within seconds, the ship was whizzing along.

For a few seconds everything went fuzzy - as though the entire universe was made out of candy floss. Astra clung on to the edge of her desk. Her mouth was dry, and it felt like someone was tickling her all over.

"Hop completed!" said Volt. "We have arrived at Mercury."

A small planet covered in red and orange clouds appeared on the screen.

"Have you been to Mercury before?" Dan asked.

Astra shook her head. "This is my first time."

"Well, if you think the weather was bad back on Earth - wait until we get down there," said Dan. "It's so hot! My hair is going to look all floppy in my new profile picture."

Astra gave a sigh and then she switched the HS Infinity's controls to manual and piloted the ship to land in the car park of the Alien Animal Zoo.

Ten minutes later, the outer doors slid open and Dan and Astra stepped out, helmets fixed to the collars of their COSMIC spacesuits. Volt wheeled out with them.

"You were correct in your prediction of hot weather, Master Dan," the robot said. "The current temperature is 42 degrees Celsius."

"Ideal for those alien animals collected from the inner planets," said Dan as they passed through the open gates to the zoo. There were no staff members around, or visitors looking in the cages. The whole place was empty.

"Not so good for those animals who come from the colder planets of the Solar System," Astra pointed out.

"Does that mean you are not a fan of zoos, Miss Astra?" asked Volt.

"Not a fan at all," Astra replied. "Locking up animals just isn't natural."

"Well, you shouldn't have too much of a problem with this place," said Dan. "There don't seem to be any animals here!"

They walked along the pathways, past fenced-off fields and cages. They were all empty.

"Why did the Chief send us here if there aren't any animals?" said Astra.

"And how am I going to get a dangerous profile picture?" demanded Dan.

Astra stopped and stared at him. "What?"

Dan produced his computer tablet from inside his spacesuit. "I thought there would be all sorts of dangerous beasts here," he said. "I was going to get my photo taken with one of them and post it on Spacebook."

"Excuse me," said a shrill voice. "Am I dangerous enough for your photo?"

Dan, Astra and Volt looked down to find a yellow and black penguin at their feet. He had an orange beak, and tufts of bright green feathers running down his back.

"The name is Pay-Pay," said the penguin. "I come from the ice moon, Europa."

"And now you're the only animal left in the zoo," said Astra, stooping to smooth Pay-Pay's feathers. "You poor little chap."

Pay-Pay pulled away. "I'm not a poor little chap!" he snapped. "I'm one of the smart ones. One of the ones who did not get captured."

"Captured?" said Dan.

"That's right," said Pay-Pay. "Follow me, and I'll introduce you to the gang." The penguin leapt into the air, flapped his flippers and took off.

"You can fly!" exclaimed Astra.

"Of course I can fly!" said Pay-Pay. "Now, come on!" The penguin led the team to a small cave near the back of the zoo.

"In here." said Pay-Pay, landing beside the cave.

Astra bent down, and led the way in. Inside the cave were some very odd-looking animals.

Pay-Pay introduced some of the alien animals. "Brubeck is a five-legged horse from Neptune, Sly is a speed sloth from Saturn and Fury is an angry badger from a Uranus moon."

"Why are you all hiding away in here?" asked Dan.

"Well," said Pay-Pay, "some old bloke landed here in a big fancy spaceship and took most of the animals. We're the ones who got away."

"Old bloke?" said Astra.

"Yeah!" snarled Pay-Pay. "I wish I could get my flippers on him in his grey cardigan and comfy slippers!"

Dan and Astra turned to face one another. "The Geezer!" they cried.

CHAPTER 3

BREAKING IN

"Is that the spaceship you saw?" Astra whispered.

The three Space Hoppers were crouching behind a snack stand, with Pay-Pay and some of the alien animals they had met in the cave.

The penguin popped his head up to look at the spaceship in front of them. "That's the one," he said. "That's where the old bloke took all the animals."

Dan pulled a pair of binoculars from his belt and looked around the edge of the snack stand. He saw a large retirement home, surrounded by a white wooden fence. In the lawn near the front door was a sign saying Shady Acres.

"It's The Geezer, alright," he said, handing the binoculars over to Astra.

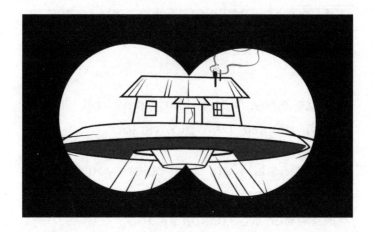

"We'll have to get closer if we want to find out what he's up to this time," said Astra. "Much closer."

"You mean inside Shady Acres itself, don't you?" said Dan. "I knew it! Going inside that place always gives me the creeps."

"I bet Captain Rocky Strong wouldn't have a problem going in there," said Astra with a sly wink to Volt. "In fact, I reckon he'd take some photographs of himself inside his enemy's hideout to post on Spacebook and prove how brave he is."

Dan was off and running towards the retirement home before Astra had finished speaking. He led the way to the back door of Shady Acres.

"Excuse me, Master Dan," said Volt. "If you will let me past, I will pick the lock."

"Okay," said Dan, "but, before you open the door, can you make it look as though I was the one who picked the lock?"

"Why would you want to do that?" asked Astra.

Dan handed his tablet to her. "It was your idea!" he said. "How great it would look if I was breaking into The Geezer's spaceship in my Spacebook profile picture!"

There was a CLICK! "We're in!" said Volt.

"Excellent!" said Dan. "Now, get out of the way so that I can pose for my picture."

"You could use this to look like a lock pick," said Pay-Pay, plucking out one of his black feathers.

"Brilliant!" said Dan. He knelt down, slid the sharp end of the feather into the keyhole, and tried to look brave.

"What are you doing?" hissed Astra.

"Looking brave." Dan hissed back.

"Well don't!" Astra hissed. "It looks like you need the toilet."

"Just take the picture!" snapped Dan.

"Alright, alright!" said Astra, raising up the tablet.

"Three, two, one ..."

Suddenly, the back door to Shady Acres swung open and a large figure appeared in the doorway.

✳ FLASH! Astra took the photograph.

"What was that?" roared the figure, rubbing his eyes. "I can't see a thing!"

"Nor can I!" said Dan, blinking hard. "The flash is too bright."

Astra looked down at the picture she had taken on the tablet. "Er ... Dan ..." she said. "I think you'd better take a look at this."

"I can't!" barked Dan. "My eyes are on fire."

"Still, I think you should look!" said Astra, turning the tablet so Dan could see it. Dan tried to focus on the picture.

It showed him kneeling at lock level, while a tall figure in a grey cardigan and comfy slippers stood over him.

"The Geezer!" he cried.

CHAPTER 4

MONSTER

Dan leapt to his feet as the Space Hoppers and the unusual animals slowly backed away.

"Dan Fireball!" snarled The Geezer.

"The Geezer!" snarled Dan Fireball.

"What are you doing here?" demanded Astra. "Where are all the animals?"

"Oh, the animals are safe, Miss Moon," said The Geezer with a wicked smile. "In fact, they're better than ever!"

"Prove it!" ordered Dan.

"Very well," said The Geezer. "I was going to wait until the morning to show off my new creation, but seeing as you are here now ... wait there!" Then The Geezer turned and went deeper into the house.

Astra took a step forward and caught the door as it began to swing closed.

"The Geezer told us to wait here!" hissed Dan.

Astra raised an eyebrow. "And you're going to listen to him?" She pulled a torch from her utility belt and stepped inside the retirement home. Dan sighed and followed.

Dan and Astra found themselves in the dark kitchen of the spaceship. They had been in here before but, this time, things looked different.

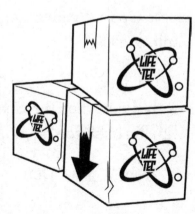

"What's in all these boxes?" asked Dan, looking at the stacks of boxes in the room.

"Looks like The Geezer has been on a shopping spree," said Astra, turning her torch to the logo on the nearest box. "Life-Tech," she read. "I've heard that name before."

"They had an advert on my Spacebook page," Dan said. "They had been working on a painless way of splicing two different kinds of animal together."

"Splicing?" said Astra.

"Yeah," said Dan. "So you could splice your hamster with a dolphin to make a hamphin that swims in the bath with you. Or you could splice a parrot with a centipede and get a walkie talkie."

"Oh dear," said Astra. "I think I've just worked out what The Geezer has been doing with the alien zoo animals!"

"What?" asked Dan.

Before Astra could reply, a monster crashed through the wall and into the kitchen. It was difficult to see in the dim light, but neither Dan nor Astra wanted to hang around to get a better look. They dashed back out of the spaceship retirement home

"RUN!" yelled Dan, sprinting away down the path.

The others didn't need telling twice. They followed quickly, just as the monster exploded out of the back of Shady Acres.

Volt spun his head dome around and looked back at the creature that was chasing them. "Oh my!" he said quietly.

The creature chasing them was a mixture of half a dozen animals or possibly more. It had the giant body of a brown bear, which had two tiger heads. The monster's legs were sabre-toothed camels, and its arms were a pair of snarling warthogs, their tusks were hissing rattlesnakes.

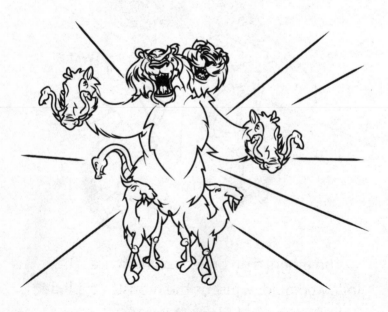

"I don't believe it!" cried Dan. "The perfect monster to have my photo taken with, and we're running away from it!"

"You want to stop and take pictures?" Astra gasped.

"The Chief won't believe us if he doesn't see a photo of this monster," panted Dan.

"You're right!" said Astra, skidding to a halt. "The Geezer has gone too far this time. We need evidence if we're going to convict him."

Dan hopped from foot to foot beside her. "I didn't mean it!" he shouted.

Astra pulled out the computer tablet and pointed the camera lens at the beast. "How do you turn the flash off?" she asked.

"JUST TAKE THE PICTURE!" shouted Dan.

35

Astra aimed the camera, focused and then screamed as the tiger heads of the monster grabbed her. Roaring loudly the monster lifted Astra high into the air.

The Geezer appeared behind his creation, a leather whip in his hand. "Don't eat her!" he ordered. "I want her in once piece when I take her hostage."

The tigers' heads growled angrily, but didn't bite down any further.

"ASTRA!" cried Dan.

"Don't worry," cried Pay-Pay. "I'll sort this!" The penguin flew up to one of the warthog arms and began to peck at it, angrily. The warthog squealed in pain and wrapped one of its snake tusks tightly around the bird.

"Quick!" said Dan, turning to Brubeck the horse. "Charge at them!"

Brubeck blew hot air from his nostrils, but instead of running straight at the legs of the monster, the horse started to run in small circles instead.

"What?" cried Dan.

"It's the extra leg, I fear," said Volt. "It looks like he can't run in a straight line."

Dan screamed in frustration and spun round one more time. All the other animals had disappeared, except for one - Fury the angry badger.

"Your turn!" Dan yelled. "Get angry!"

The badger snarled, spat, gnashed its teeth and then pulled out a notepad and a pen and began to write quickly.

Dan couldn't believe his eyes. "What's he doing?"

"Writing a letter to the editor of his local newspaper," cried Pay-Pay . "It's how he gets rid of his anger!"

Dan looked back up at Astra. "I can't help you!" he called.

"It's Okay," shouted Astra. "I don't blame you. But, you have to do this …" She threw Dan's tablet back down to him. "Take pictures and show them to the Chief. Use them as evidence against The Geezer."

Dan raised the tablet, aimed the camera lens at the snarling monster, and pressed the button.

 FLASH!

Suddenly, the monster began to whirl around, screaming in pain.

"It's the camera flash, Dan!" yelled Astra. "It's scaring the monster. Keep taking photographs."

Dan raised the tablet again.

FLASH!

FLASH!

Volt slid out a very old camera from a slot in his side and joined in with the photography.

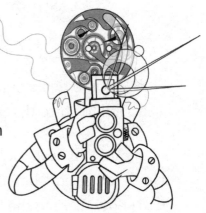

✳ FLASH! ✳

✳ FLASH! ✳

✳ FLASH! ✳

The monster stumbled backwards. The snake holding Pay-Pay let him go, and the penguin flew up to the tigers' mouths. He began to peck again and again at the tigers' noses.

"Come on!" he shouted. "Let her go!"

✳ FLASH! ✳

✳ FLASH! ✳

✳ FLASH! ✳

At last the tigers opened their mouths and Astra fell towards the path below.

Pay-Pay swooped down and caught the collar of her spacesuit in his beak, setting her down on the ground very carefully.

"Thank you," Astra cried, hugging the penguin tightly.

"Any time," said Pay-Pay. "But we're not safe yet!"

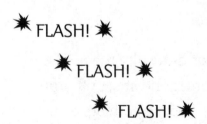

Dan and Volt continued to terrify the spliced-together monster with their cameras. The beast closed all of its eyes and backed away.

"Where are you going?" screamed The Geezer. "Get back there and attack the Space Hoppers!" He swung out with the whip, catching one of the tigers on its cheek.

That was the final straw for the beast. It turned on The Geezer, and began to advance.

"No! NO!" cried The Geezer. "Leave me alone. I *made* you!"

But any feelings of loyalty the monster once had were long gone. It set off after The Geezer as he fled, screaming, across the empty zoo.

Back on board the HS Infinity, Volt finished a video call with the Chief and wheeled over to where Dan was bandaging the scratches on Astra's arms and legs.

"I'm afraid The Geezer has managed to escape capture once again," said the robot. "Shady Acres took off a little over ten minutes ago."

"What, even with that big hole in the wall?" said Dan.

"Its power was limited," said Volt, "but that did not stop The Geezer reaching light speed before the Chief could get another Space Hopper team there."

"What about the monster?" asked Astra.

"Luckily, The Geezer didn't want to take it with him," said Volt. "Another Space Hopper team will tranquilize it, and then they will call for vets to un-splice the various animals and return them to their cages."

"Another Space Hopper team?" said Dan. "You don't mean ..."

"Captain Rocky Thunder and his crew, I'm afraid." said Volt.

"Typical!" Dan sighed. Something pinged in Astra's pocket. She pulled out her smartphone and peered at the screen. "Hey, look!" she said. "Rocky Thunder has added me as a friend on Spacebook. He says my profile picture makes me look really dangerous!"

Dan took the phone from her. Astra's picture was one of the photographs he had taken of her clamped in the monster's twin tiger mouths.

"I told you this planet was unbearable," he groaned.

THE END

Now read *Endgame on Earth* to find out what The Geezer gets up to next!

GLOSSARY

advance – to come towards

editor – a person who puts articles together to make a newspaper

hostage – someone held prisoner by one person to make another person do what they want

manual – being controlled by a human rather than a computer

splicing – to join together

spree – a busy time doing lots of one activity

tranquilize – to calm down or relax something, usually with an injection or other medicine

utility belt – belt for carrying a range of tools and equipment

QUIZ QUESTIONS

1   What is Dan taking photos for?

2   Why was the Hop Drive not working?

3   What is the temperature on Mercury when they arrive?

4   What sort of animal is Brubeck?

5   What has The Geezer done on Mercury?

6   What is the name of The Geezer's spaceship retirement home?

7   What have Life-Tech been working on?

8   How many tiger heads does the monster have?

9   What effect does the camera flash have on the monster?

10 Why did the monster turn on The Geezer?

ABOUT THE AUTHOR

Tommy Donbavand writes full-time and lives in Lancashire with his family. He is also the author of the 13-book *Scream Street* series (currently in production for TV) and has written numerous books for children and young adults.

For Tommy, the best thing about being an author is getting to spend his days making up adventures for his readers. He also writes for 'The Bash Street Kids' in *The Beano*, which excites him beyond belief!

Find out more about Tommy and his other books at www.tommydonbavand.com

QUIZ ANSWERS

1   Spacebook
2   It had worn down cables.
3   42 degrees Celsius
4   A five-legged horse from Neptune
5   He has kidnapped all the animals from the zoo.
6   Shady Acres
7   A painless way to splice to animals together.
8   Two
9   It whirls around and cries out in pain.
10 Because he hit it with his whip.